LIES IN THE EYES

MANYA SHARMA

Made with ♥ on the Notion Press Platform
www.notionpress.com

This book is dedicated to my parents, who introduced me to the world of literature and my dear sister Kamya Sharma who gave depth to my imagination.

Contents

Love doesn't find reasons to leave, it finds the reasons to stay.
How strange love is......
It's everywhere yet the hardest to find.
It's in the wind
It's in the rain
It's in the wound
And in the pain...

Manya Sharma

ACKNOWLEDGEMENTS

I gave words to my dream of writing this book but, I would like to thank the people who gave this dream its wings and sky to fly and made it a reality.
My sincere thanks to my father, for his support and suggestions while I was writing this book.
I would like to thank my mother and my sisters for motivating me and for being such wonderful readers.

I

The Attraction

Dazzling moon, the pleasing wind, love and light everywhere. Everyone was so lost in the party that day, music and dance were going on all around, the new year party was having a blast.

Everyone was dancing and then she saw a guy standing at the side of the dance floor watching everyone silently with a smile.

God! What a good looking person. Tall, muscular, dark brown mysterious eyes, quite similar to the freshly wet soil, the most attractive hands and charming smile. Moreover, his eyes weren't just beautiful but very lively too, very expressive. It was really hard not to notice him.

Hey Aaisha! Come, allow me to introduce you to someone.

Chirag took Aaisha to introduce her to that man who's his friend.

Aaisha, this is Arnav, one of my closest friends, and Arnav this is Aaisha, she's one of my closets too.

Hello Aaisha! You're looking gorgeous.

Hello Arnav! Thank you so much, you're looking great too.

You know what guys? You can stare at each other all night long. I 'm gonna see if everyone is doing okay at the party.

Chirang teased Arnav with a look and went back.

Arnav looked her in the eyes and said, "You have such a lovely smile."

She smiled and said, "well, I was about to say the same thing to appreciate your eyes."

He smiled and was still looking into her eyes. I'm Glad you noticed.

His deep voice and his charm was enough to grab much attention at the party.

By the way, Arnav, why were you standing alone here?

Because Sometimes even the crowd can't take away the emptiness.

Aaisha felt something strange in those words then suddenly, he smiled at her and said, "uh! well I was just kidding. Actually I didn't have someone to dance with, maybe because I suck at dancing."

Uh oh! Really? Well we all are terrible dancers here.

Oh well Aaisha, then I won't mind dancing if you would care to join me for a dance.

Ah that smirk! Well I can't say no to that.

He asked for her hand very gently.

May I?

Sure! she smiled.

He took her to the dance floor, slow and romantic music was playing in the background, he held her from the waist to make her come slightly closer. He moved close to her neck.

you smell really nice.

She looked at him and then broke eye contact.

Uh! Thank you.

He could see how nervous she was.

Both were still dancing and then music stopped.

Hey guys! may I have your attention please

Chirag asked everyone to enjoy the meal.

"Hey buddy! What's going on? You are

looking happy."

Sid and Shruti asked Arnav.

I don't know, I am just feeling good today.

Well Arnav, is Aaisha the reason for it?

They all laughed teasing him.

Hey come on, I barely know her.

Then he looked at her.

All I know is her name but yes her smile is calming. And her aura is so attractive that it's hard for anyone to not look at her or it's hard for me to not stare and admire how amazing she seems to me. She's gorgeous.

Um I.. I mean.

He realised that he's saying it in front of all his friends, he was so lost in her.

"Oh my god! Our handsome guy is into her

isn't he?" Shruti said excitedly.

Hey you guys don't do that ok? You all know I am not ready for it.

But Arnav, it's the first time in months that you are genuinely looking happy around someone because most of the time you just pretend it.

Guys I think... I don't know. Let's just enjoy today, and talk about it some other time.

Yup as your wish buddy. Let's hit the floor again then.

They all moved to the dance floor again.

He went to the garden and bumped into Aaisha.

Ouch!

Oh I am so sorry, are you okay?

No problem Arnav, I am ok.

I didn't know you were here Aaisha... by the way why are you here?

Actually music was very loud inside and I had to pick an urgent call. What about you?

Um actually, I just needed some air.

oh? Is everything okay?

Yeah I'm fine.

Ok then I should leave, bye.

Uh wait Aaisha! You can.. you can stay here.

Sure?

Yes!

Alright, actually I am feeling better here too, I don't really drink that much so I guess I can stay here until they are done with it and look at the sky, so beautiful, I can stare at it all night.

That's..that's different.

Different? Hahaha well, should I consider it as a compliment Arnav?

Hahaha yes of course, I mean I usually don't see people who look at even the casual things with such excitement. Maybe that's the reason I don't get on well with everyone so quickly.

Well I really love to spend time staring at the moon or just by feeling the wind, I feel so lively.

That's beautiful Aaisha. Do you like music or anything like that?

Oh I can't tell you how much I love it, I can't spend a day without it. What about you?

Yes I do. I love music too.Well I think we can sit here and then talk.

Yeah sure.

They both sat on the chairs in the garden, she was looking at the moon calmly, the wind was slightly cold. He was still just looking at her.

Arnav, are you gonna stare at me like this all the time?

Uh I'm sorry it is just that you're beautiful.

She looked at him and smiled.

They talked, talked and talked. Party was still on but they didn't feel the need to go in.

Oh! It's 2AM already? I got to go home.

2AM? I didn't realise where the time went by,

Should I drop you home?

No, that's so sweet of you but I will manage.

Chirag will drive me back home.

Sure?

Yes!

Ok it was really nice talking to you Aaisha.

Same here Arnav. Bye bye!

Bye!

What a beautiful day it was, she never felt so comfortable with talking to a complete stranger.

II

Something Unsaid

Here's your order ma'am, have a good day.

Thank you so much.

Oh what? Is it Arnav?

Aaisha saw Arnav while stepping out of the coffee shop.

He was sitting alone and was writing something in a diary. Was looking a bit lost.

Hey Arnav!

Oh hi aaisha! What a surprise.

Actually I was just leaving when I saw you here, I thought I should say hello at least.

Yes you did right, come sit, let's have a coffee then.

I would love to but I think you must be expecting someone here, so we can grab a coffee some other day.

Oh no, I am not expecting anyone here.

Are you sure?

Yes! And I would love to have a coffee with you.

Ok then. Hey by the way, do you mind if I ask what's that diary?

Um actually most of the time when I don't have anyone to listen to me, I love to write it down. It makes me feel better.

Wow this is nice, but.

But?

Nothing I was wondering how can someone not listen to you? You're such a nice person to talk to.

Thanks. But there are times when people have so much to say and they know others will struggle to understand.

Things which are hidden in heart and things which eyes express.

Well anyway, I think I should not bore you on our first coffee together.

I don't think I can be bored with you so don't worry. In fact, I would say whenever you feel like no one's here to listen, you can always talk to me.

He smiled and said, "you don't know how much these words mean to me."

They spend around an hour talking to each other.

Ok Arnav, thank you so much for the coffee. It was so good to meet you here.

He looked at her with a smile and said, "thank you for giving me company here. Bye!"

She felt something, something unusual, she saw a totally different person in him, a person who was not as happy as he looks.

He saw something different in her, a supportive person, a listener, someone who has so much respect towards everyone's feelings, someone caring, loving and beautiful.

His phone rang.

Hi Arjun!

Hey Chirag! How are you?

Am good. Actually, I saw you with Aaisha today, and I couldn't stop myself from calling you. See I know you don't like to rush into relationships or even friendship but Arnav

I don't remember when was the last time I saw you smiling like this, I want to tell you that she is one of the best people I have ever seen.

Chirag, brother I know you guys want to see me happy and I totally agree with the fact that she's the best. But you know what I am worried about? If I am good for her or not. She is indeed the most beautiful person but that's the reason, I feel like why will she ever be with someone like me, so for now I think we should be friends only.

Ok Arnav, I will not force you for anything but you're not the wrong guy for her, I know you, and I know you're a person with a heart of gold. But anyway, it's your call. By the way, I will call you back later, I have got to go somewhere.

Yeah sure, bye!

It's been more than a week since I saw her but her pure eyes and smile is something I can't get my mind off, the first time in months or maybe in years someone made me feel that I am not alone and they are here to listen to me whenever I feel lonely. Those words might be something normal to say to someone for a kind hearted person like her, but for me those words were like a raindrop in the desert.

His phone was in his hand and he really wanted to message her, he wanted to hear her voice again. After stopping himself for hours, he ended up messaging her.

Hey Aaisha!

Oh hi! How have you been?

Great! I hope my message didn't disturb you.

No, not at all. It's nice that you messaged. I was thinking about you.

Really? You were? Is it allowed for a guy to blush?

Hahaha, well I won't mind.

Hahaha, actually I was thinking of taking you to dinner if you are okay with it Aaisha.

Oh! A dinner?

Yes! Tomorrow.

Um, actually I have some work tomorrow but we can go out the day after tomorrow if that suits you.

Sure! I will pick you up at 8.

Ok, see you...

Woah... what am I doing? Did I really ask her out? Why do I wanna see her again and again. I hope I am not rushing into it.

Oh my god! Did I really say yes to have a dinner with him? What am I doing? Is it too early or is it the way it should be? Maybe I'm thinking too much about it, it's just a simple dinner.

Oh god! What should I wear? I don't know what she'll like for me to wear to the dinner today? Damn! I have never been that nervous just for a simple dinner. What is wrong with me?

Her phone rang! It's him.

I don't know why am I getting so nervous to go out with him? Aah! I should pick up his call.

Hello!

Hi, are you ready? actually am just outside your house to pick you up.

Oh, are you here already? That's so sweet of you, I am ready. Wait, I am coming outside.

He was standing outside looking absolutely amazing in that black shirt, and brown trousers. As always his eyes were saying a lot but all he was wearing on his face was the most beautiful and pure smile. He was holding a box of chocolates in his hand, oh my god! His hands are so wonderful, his well builded arms and veiny hands, his masculinity was visible through his well builded physique. His dark brown hair, he looked like an absolute gentleman. I couldn't take my eyes off him.

She came out of her house, and I was just stunned looking at her, her untied beautiful long hair, her shining bright eyes, her beautiful lips and that red lipstick was just looking amazing on her, her smile was as always the most beautiful thing, that black dress was wonderful and she had something in her hand. Her inner beauty was well reflected on her face.

I opened the car door for her, but couldn't take my eyes off her. She gave me a beautiful smile and thanked me for holding the door. She sat in the car, and I started driving. I was so nervous I didn't know what to say to her.

You are looking beautiful, Aaisha.

Thank you so much Arnav, you're looking good too, black suits you.

Thank you so much. I am happy that you agreed to have dinner with me, it's a pleasure for me.

Hey, the pleasure is all mine.

Here we reached Aaisha.

Then he opened the car door for her, asked her to hold his hand, and took her to the table.

Please sit.

Thank you.

Oh no, I was so nervous that I forgot to give you these chocolates I bought for you, you told me at that party you like chocolates. I hope you will like it.

Thank you so much, I love these chocolates. And I think we are feeling the same, I bought something too and forgot to give it to you.

That's so sweet of you. Let me open it.

Oh! It's... it's us. Our photo, who clicked it?

Um actually I asked Chirag to share the pictures of that party then I found it in those pictures. So, I thought why not frame it and give it to you, after all it's our first picture together.

There's something written on this frame,

It says, "I am here for you". It's....

Did you not like it?

No I loved it, I can't tell you how much, it's one of the best gifts I have ever received. This is beautiful. Am just a bit emotional with this message written on this frame.these words mean a lot to me.

I am glad you liked it.

His teary eyes were making me feel confused, why would someone feel so emotional with such a small gift?

Is there something that he hasn't told me yet about himself?

Um, I think we should start the dinner now, the food is looking delicious.

Oh sure!

Her presence was enough to make me feel the happiest. Listening to her, talking to her, seeing her laugh, smile and blush on my compliments was just the best feeling, but why am I getting so attached to her? And that gift of hers.... how easily and beautifully she said that something that no one did through that quote on the frame. And our photo, it was just beyond beautiful.

How easily she lifts up everyone's mood, how beautifully she supports people around her, it's the first time I met someone who actually admires feelings, who admires every small thing around, who doesn't show it but has the most kind heart, who is capable of finding beauty in everything. Whose presence can make a person like me feel better, I didn't realise how happy I started to feel around her. After a really long time I didn't have to pretend to be anything, I was literally being myself and she was ok with it. She's a person who has boundaries yet is compassionate.

We finished the food and it was time to leave, though I wanted her to stay a bit longer but it was already late and I didn't have enough courage to ask her to stay, I got up and held her hand while leaving from there, her hand in mine was totally a different feeling, we sat in the car she turned on the music, I was feeling that every line of the songs was about her. Neither of us talked as I could clearly see her getting nervous as much as I was. We reached her home and I stepped out of the car to open her side of the door but there was something inside me that didn't want her to go.

Her inner beauty as well as her angel like appearance, everything was kind of making it hard for me to leave. It was a little windy too, her hair was bothering her left eye, so I placed them behind her ear but she wasn't looking at me. Clearly, she was blushing, I could sense her breathing a little heavier. I went a bit closer, she looked into my eyes with a certain nervousness on her face. I held her from her waist, she slightly placed one of her hands on my chest and the other on my shoulder. I could feel her fingers on the back of my neck holding me tightly.

We kissed, kissed and kissed. I was so lost in her I wasn't able to think about anything at that moment. She slowly stepped back and was blushing so much.

She wasn't looking at me but I was staring at her, I didn't realise that it was making her more nervous.

She gave me a small hug and whispered good night in my ear, smiled again and went inside her house. I was standing there and was just smiling and then I drove back home, though I was just thinking about her all along the way.

Oh my god! Did we? Did we just kiss?

He kissed me? I still can't tell if it was a dream or real. His hand on my waist, his pure and deep eyes which were staring at me. I didn't know what I just did, I just got lost in him. This was one of the best moments for me. I don't know what he feels about me but I want to know what is this? that I feel when I see him, why does his presence make me happy, why do I feel so safe around him? Why does his stare make me blush so much?

Maybe I am thinking way too much, I should probably go to sleep now. But I wish he could stay a bit longer with me.

III

The Storm

Hey Aaisha! I am feeling feverish today so I can't join you in the gym, I am sorry.

Oh it's completely fine Shruti, take care of yourself and get well soon.

It was 6 in the evening. Aaisha went to the gym but surprisingly, there weren't many people in the gym.

Great, no crowd in the gym today!

Aaisha? Hi!

Arnav? You? Here?

Yes, actually the gym that I go to was closed today. So, I came here and I think I got lucky with the timing.

Hahaha! What a good coincidence, it's nice to see you. Texting and calling were making me miss you a little more than usual.

Oh really? I think I was feeling the same. I really wanted to see you but I thought you might think that I am just being too much.

Hey i don't judge that much, ok let's complete the workout first then we can spend some time together.

I don't know what is happening, wherever I go I find him. I don't know what I am feeling, this is something I never felt before. When he's with me I don't want the day to end. When I think about him I want to stop the time, this wind, this moon, this weather. Why do I feel him in everything?

Everything he says feels so true to me.

Hey?

Yes!

Are you done with the workout Aaisha? only we are left in the gym.

Oh yes, I am done, let's go.

He opened the door and he could barely see anything, there was a blizzard going on. He immediately closed the door.

Oh god! What's this? How are we gonna go home in this weather Arnav?

Exactly!

He messaged Chirag to ask if he could do something as he lives nearby the gym.

Hello Arnav, I am so sorry I am out of town and I just saw the news and they are asking everyone to be at a safe place or find a safe place as soon as possible to be at, until the weather gets clear.

Oh what? But Aaisha is here with me too. Where are we gonna go then?

Aaisha is there too? Keep her safe buddy. There is a hotel near the gym, try to reach there if possible, and stay there. Try to Get a room quickly as most of the hotels are full because of the weather.

Uh ok I will try to find a place.

Aaisha! We have to find a hotel or something to stay at tonight as roads are getting blocked because of the weather and it is asked to not go on roads.

Oh my god! Ok let's find a place then.

He held her hand and they stepped outside the gym. It was insanely cold there but they managed to get into the hotel which was just within walking distance from the gym.

Hello sir! How may I help you?

Hello! Actually We need two rooms.

We are sorry sir, we only have one room available today due to the weather.

Uh! Ok. Aaisha, can you please check how far the other hotels will be if we try to go.

Ok, um no... There are some hotels but they are far from this hotel. The nearest hotel is a two hour drive from here. We can't drive in this weather.

What should we do now? Are you okay with us staying in the same room?

Umm, we don't have a choice, I am ok.

Sure? Should I get it?

Yes.

Excuse me, I would like to have this room....

Our room was on the second floor, we were in the elevator, I could see she was not that comfortable but there wasn't any other choice.

We entered the room, it was so beautiful. Somewhere, I was happy because I couldn't ask for anything better than being able to spend time with her.

Her hands were freezing, we were in the gym, we clearly did not have anything warm to wear. However, The temperature in the room was warm so I asked her to put on the blanket.

She went to have a warm shower first.

Being with her is a blessing itself, her presence can not be described in words. I couldn't take my mind off the fact that how lucky that party was for me. I met Aaisha there for the first time and since then my life has been completely changed. I have started to be normal, to be genuinely happy, I started being myself, and she is the one who never judged me.

Arnav! Do you wanna use the shower? I am done now.

Oh hey, how are you feeling now?

Much better. I was freezing at that time.

Ok, I think I need a shower too.

He took a shower too and came back while Aaisha was combing her hair. As always she was looking absolutely gorgeous.

You're looking beautiful.

She was facing the mirror, she turned and looked at him.

Thank you Arnav. Such an unusual day huh? I never thought I would be here with you today.

But Aaisha, I would say I am lucky.

His intense eye contact was making her blush again.

She turned back towards the mirror but I could see her smiling.

We ordered dinner and talked about so many things. but, I could only remember her smile. I don't know what this feeling is.

Arnav, I am gonna go to sleep now, I am drained. Good night.

Good night Aaisha.

I layed on one side of the bed and she on the other. We both were nervous. Was Chirag and everyone else right? Am I falling for her? No, I can't let this happen. I just can't. It's wrong.

I should do something before the situation slips out of my hands. I took it too far. I should stop it all, right here. She doesn't know anything about...

She opened her eyes slowly, and looked at me. She smiled.

Good morning Arnav.

Good morning.

I hope you slept comfortably last night.

Yes, I did.

What happened? Arnav, you are not looking okay.

I'm absolutely fine, I wanna leave. I have some work.

Get ready, I will drop you to your home.

Uh ok.

I was still wondering what happened to him suddenly? He was in such a good mood last night and right now he's behaving like he wants to get rid of me.

Arnav, am ready we can go now.

Ok sure.

He didn't say a single word all the way.

Bye Arnav! Thank you so much for....

No problem.

He didn't even let me finish the sentence and went back without saying a bye or anything.

I don't know why this behaviour is hurting me? I never let anyone come close to me in such a short period of time. I felt something, maybe a connection with him. But I don't know what went wrong suddenly. He was on my mind all day long, I couldn't stop thinking about why he was behaving so strangely with me.

Hello Arnav, sorry to call you at such a late hour but I just wanted to ask if everything is ok or not. because you were not in a good mood today.

Hello Aaisha, I am fine, I don't know what you expect from me to behave but that's me. It was just a normal behaviour of mine. You can stop wasting your time thinking about my mood.

But Arnav I was just worri..

Arnav?

He cut the call. But why is behaving like a stranger to me?

It feels like I don't even know this person.

Maybe he needs some space.

I didn't message or call him for a week or two, neither did he.

Hey Aaisha!

Hello Chirag!

How have you been lately, Aaisha? Is everything ok? It's been days. You didn't message or call me. I was getting worried.

I am fine Chirag. I am glad you asked. I was missing you all guys.

Great, then let's meet. We all are here at my house. Join us please.

Ok great. I am coming then.

Hey Chirag!

Heyyy... it's so good to see you Aaisha. Come inside, we all were waiting for you.

Hey Arnav? Where are you going?

Chirag I have some urgent work today. I will catch you later.

Ok, but you can at least say hi to Aaisha.

I don't think that's important for any of us.

He left. He didn't even look at me. He was absolutely fine and I was worried about him all this time.

Aaisha? Are you... are you crying?

No, I am ok Chirag.

Aaisha what happened between you guys? You both were so good just a couple of days ago.

Nothing happened, Shruti. Can we please talk about something else?

Ok sure.

Everyone could sense that nothing was fine between them, but Aaisha was already looking hurt. So, no one asked anything related to Arnav. They spent a day together and made her feel a little better.

Aaisha started to try to take her mind off things but she was still confused about what happened to Arnav suddenly. Another week passed and they didn't talk.

IV
The Touch

Arnav's phone rang.

Hello! Yes Shruti.

Hello Arnav, can you please tell me what's wrong with you? Why are you behaving like this to her?

To whom?

You know exactly whom I'm talking about. How can you be so heartless with her? First you let her come close, you made her feel that you really like her and suddenly, one day you started behaving like a stranger and now you're being so heartless, you didn't even go to see her to the hospital.

Hospital? Aaisha is in hospital? What...What happened to her? Is she fine? Why is she in the hospital?

As if you don't know?

No, I don't. We haven't talked for days.

Oh god! Seriously, I can't believe it. Aaisha fell from the stairs and her leg got hurt badly. She has been in the hospital for days. We all go to see her daily and you haven't even messaged her?

Shruti, will you please give the address of that hospital? I wanna see her. Please.

Ok. Let me send you the address on the text, bye.

Ok.

He rushed to see her, as if his heart stopped beating, tears were rolling out of his eyes.

Aaisha! Aaisha!

Arnav?

Chirag, where's Aaisha? Is this her room? Is she here?

Yes. Arnav, she's here. Go, see her.

Aaisha!

Ar...Arnav?

Yes, what happened? Are you ok now? I am so sorry, I didn't know you were here baby. Are you fine now? Aaisha?

"Yes, I am better. It's good to see you here, Arnav." She said in a low voice.

He kissed her forehead.

Why didn't you tell me that you're in the hospital?

I thought you don't want to talk to me. I didn't want to force anything on you. I didn't want to be a burden on you.

Burden? Aaisha you know nothing, it's me who's being a burden on you. Who's hurting you. Anyways, it's not the right time to talk about that. How many days do you have to stay here?

I can go home tomorrow. Just a little weakness is all I am feeling now. Otherwise, I am much better now.

Are you sure?

I am.

May I stay here today? Please.

I am feeling better Arnav, you don't have to waste your time here.

Please Aaisha, I want to stay with you today.

Arnav, I don't know what is this, what's true and what is not. But I don't want to feel the way I felt in the past few weeks. I can not understand what is in your mind, it feels like I don't know you, as if there are two different people. One is caring, loving and expressive, who makes sure that I am fine and then there's this person who doesn't even want to talk to me or see my face, who doesn't even care about me. I don't want to face all this trouble again Arnav, it might be... be.

Aaisha? Don't stress please, take this, drink some water please.

He helped her to sit and drink some water.

Are you ok now?

Arnav, I was saying it might mean nothing to you but it hurts me. So it's better for us to maintain a gap.

He was listening to it all and was just staring at her, lost in some thoughts.

Arnav? Are you not gonna say anything?

I.. I know I messed up but... but Aaisha there are reasons, it's not what you see, it's not who I am. There's a lot more you are unaware of and Aaisha please let me be with you until you're fine again. I promise, I will not bother you if you don't want to see me again.

She looked at him with eyes full of tears and words she wanted to say but all she said was...

"Ok. If you want, you can stay."

Then, he suddenly hugged her. They both were trying to hold their tears but could not hold them much longer.

Arnav, but there's a condition. I want to know what is this that you're talking about? Is there anything that I don't know?

Aaisha! I will, I will tell you everything but not now. You need rest.. I want you to get better first.

Ok, if you want, we can talk about it later.

I don't know what is going on, I wanted her to stay away from me but, when she was away, it felt like I lost my world.

I lost a chance to be a normal person again.

He sat beside her.

Hold my hand, we are going home.

Her eyes were enough to make me understand how much I had hurt her, how much she's confused about my behaviour and how kind she is.

She wasn't able to stand, but did not want my help either. I knew she would not say that she needed my help. So I didn't ask her anything...

Arnav? Hey, what are you doing ?

Picking you up, so that you don't have to walk to the car, I will take you to the car and do not ask me to put you down.

He picked me up, staying close to him is one of the best feelings in the world.

Feeling his hands on my body and holding him as if he belongs to me. Only me. I don't know where is it all going, despite of what has been going on since days, I was feeling complete with him, I knew I felt something for him. Maybe all I feel is just for him.

His intense look, his care, his voice. Why can't I stay away from these? Why does a guy I met a few months ago mean so much to me now, why does it not bother me when he comes close to me, when he holds me.

He took me to the car and made me sit in it. He made sure I was comfortable.

I know I messed up, one day I kissed you and after few days I acted like I don't know you. But all I can tell you now is that it wasn't your fault. You did nothing wrong Aaisha. In Fact when I look at you all I want is to keep you with me to kiss you, to hug you, to......

To?

To... to make love to you, and never let you go, to own every inch of your body, to feel you.

We have reached Arnav!

Huh?

We have reached my home. You can stop the car here.

I had no words to reply to what he just said, he stepped out of the car, came to my side, then opened the car door, he came closer, to pick me up. I had no control on what I was feeling. For a moment, I forgot about what happened in the past few days. All I could see was him close to me, close enough to make me feel his warm breath.

I picked her up. It wasn't easy for me to control to not kiss her, but somehow, I managed to take her to her bedroom and I took her to the bed. It was time for me to leave but something was stopping me, her touch was all I wanted to feel, her scent was all I wanted to smell.

Lights were off. He sat beside me, he placed one hand on my right thigh, his hands were cold, he slightly slid his hand a little up to have a grip of my skin and then, he pulled me closer. I could do nothing but grab the bedsheet in my hand slowly.

I could feel his warm breath on my neck and before I could say anything, he slowly kissed me there.

She was breathing heavily, her body was reacting on every touch of mine, I kissed her on the side of neck, she closed her eyes, her skin was warm, I looked her in the eyes, I could sense her heart beating faster, she slowly placed her hand on a side of my face, she slowly pulled me to her, came closer, closer and closer. We couldn't help it but kissed, her touch was making me feel the burn in every part of my body.

She then slightly kissed my cheek before sliding back. I saw her opening her eyes slowly, even her nervousness was making me fall in love with her all over again.

She looked away and I could see my stare making her blush as always.

I stood up and bent a little bit to kiss her on the forehead before leaving.

Take care Aaisha. I am just a call away if you need anything.

She nodded and said, "Thank you." In a low voice.

Her smile was working like a cure to me, ahh! It's hard for me to go but I know things will lead to something that she might not be ready for yet. If I stayed.

I went out of her home, It was windy and cold. It suddenly reminded me of the night we stayed together due to the weather. The night where I had a chance to say how I feel about her.

He left, I wanted him to stay with me but I didn't have enough courage to ask him to stay. How will I ever be able to tell him what I feel for him, how much he mean to me?

Hello! Aaisha?

Hi shruti!

How are you feeling now? I heard Arnav dropped you at your home.

Um yes he did. I am fine now all thanks to you guys. You took care of me so well.

Hey, it's fine and it's good to see things getting better between you both.

Actually Shruti I don't know what is going on.. the person who was with me today, he was caring, loving and sweet. But the person I was dealing with a couple weeks ago was someone who didn't even want to talk to me. You tell me who I should believe.

Aaisha, I don't know what went wrong but I do know that he is not a bad person. I think you guys should talk it out.

Well, I was thinking the same thing that maybe talking to him will help me in deciding what I should do.

Yes! So get better first and then clear it.

Shruti was right and even I feel that there isn't anything that can not be solved through communication. I will talk to him about it after a few days.

Her phone rang...it's his name on the screen. ARNAV.

Hey Aaisha, Arnav here. How are you feeling today? Is your leg okay now?

Hello Arnav! I am perfectly fine now, and thank you so much, you keep a check on me by taking out time to call me daily.

Come on! Aaisha. Talking to you and making sure you're fine is what makes me feel better.

Arnav, can I ask something from you?

Sure Aaisha.

Can we meet tomorrow? Do you remember? you promised me that you would tell me what is that you are hiding.

Uh, Aaisha.... ok. Take care, I will meet you tomorrow at the same place where we first went for dinner. at 7PM

I couldn't sleep the whole night. I was thinking about Arnav, what he would say, what he didn't tell me yet.

It's 6PM already.

I was really blank. I called him before heading to the restaurant.

V
Heart to Heart

Hello Aaisha!

Arnav? What happened? You're sounding so low. Is everything ok?

Yes I am feeling a little feverish. But don't worry I will reach there on time.

Are you out of your mind? A little feverish? Really? Your voice is clearly indicating something else. You stay there, I am coming.

No Aaisha, you don't have to worry. Really, I am fine.

Arnav, please.

I was so worried, I rushed to him.

He opened the door. He was looking so weak, I touched his forehead to feel his temperature.

Are you serious Arnav? You have a high fever. Come with me and sit here.

She held my hand and took me to the couch. I sat down and she was looking so worried.

Aaisha, don't worry I will be fine.

Let me check your temperature first, and do you even know how weak you're looking today?

I am sorry I spoiled our dinner.

Arnav, seriously? Do you think that even matters to me right now? You are all that matters to me.

Umm, I mean you are.. you're more important than a dinner plan.

Her shyness makes me fall in love with her more and more.

Oh my god! Your temperature is so high, have you taken any medicine? I think we should see a doctor.

Actually I consulted a doctor and I have taken the medicine that he asked me to, but I don't know why my body is aching so much.

Yes, because you are still having a fever but it's good that you already took the medicine. I think you should take a rest, you can go to your room and relax. I will cook something for us.

Hey, don't bother yourself. I can cook for us Aaisha.

Arnav please, do as I say, look at yourself. Do you think I will let you do anything in this condition?

Ok as you say sweetheart.

He smiled, and like always his smile was one of the best things I saw.

She went into the kitchen to make something for me. I was feeling very dizzy but I thought it might stress her so I didn't tell her. I didn't realise when I dozed off while she was still in the kitchen.

Arnav! Arnav!

Uh.. my head.

What happened? Are you ok?

Yes it's just a headache.

Ok do one thing, eat something then I will massage your head, you might feel better.

She helped me to sit on the bed then she sat next to me as I wasn't in the condition to sit properly, I leaned back against the bed. She fed me with her hands.

Do you want anything else?

No just...just be here with me.

Ok then lay down I will massage your head...

Her hands were magic, she started massaging my head and every touch of hers was magical. I was feeling much better. I felt so comfortable that I dozed off again. When I woke up I saw her still sitting beside me and was still massaging my head.

Aaisha? Are you serious, you're still awake. I think you should sleep too and see, my headache is gone and my temperature is normal now. I am feeling much better now.

Ok, if you are feeling better, then I can sleep. Call me whenever you need anything.

Are you going somewhere?

Yes I am going to the other room.

Uh ok.

She was in the same house but I still wanted her to stay even closer to me. As usual, I could not ask her to be in my room. I was feeling much better but I couldn't sleep. Everything was messed up in my head, everything she needed to know, everything that I didn't tell her. Everything.

Is he still awake? I should ask him if he needs anything.

I got up because of some voices coming from Arnav's room. I went to ask him if he's alright or not but...

Is this Arnav? The door of his room was open. He was facing the other side of the room, sitting on the chair near his bed and had a guitar in his hand. He was singing.

Arnav never told me he could sing so well. His voice was amazing! I couldn't believe for a minute that it was him. But there was so much pain in his voice, a loneliness in those lyrics. Which I never heard before. He was so good that I didn't want him to stop singing so I was still standing near the entrance of the room.

Aaisha! Oh I am sorry I didn't know you were awake? Or did I wake you up by the Noise?

You call it noise? Arnav, I can not tell you how talented you are. This is wonderful. I have never heard someone sing so well. Yet you never told me about it. Why?

Uh well, you liked it?

Loved it. By the way, which song is this? I never heard it before, this is so deep, every line reflects so much pain so beautifully.

Umm actually, it isn't any song.

What? Did you?

Yes! I wrote it.

Woah! really? Arnav, you must be kidding me? Wow. This is awesome. I can't believe it.

Thank you so much Aaisha. You are the first one who heard it.

Arnav, these are so deep and intense.

Uh yeah! actually, I usually don't have anyone to listen to me so I write it and sometimes just sing it to feel better.

She was just looking at him for a minute and said, "I don't know if i should praise you for this amazing talent or should I just ask you what's hidden in those deep words..."

I'm wondering too... What is this comfort I feel when you look at me the way you're looking at me right now.

She immediately Looked down. Clearly, she was feeling shy.

Is everything ok Arnav? You don't look happy sometimes.

He Smiled a bit and said "You're the first one to notice... Actually, There are things I don't know how to say. A strange feeling hits me whenever I remember my past."

Past? What happened..?

Just ignore what I said. I don't want to burden you with all the bad stuff

And wait, lemme make coffee for us. ok?

He left the room. She followed him to the kitchen.

Hey, do you really think that I'd be bothered with anything that you will share? Is that how much you know me? Arnav, I am here with you at midnight to make sure you're fine. Don't you think that's what any friendship or relationship is all about? Making sure that we all are fine and happy.

He was just staring at her with teary eyes.

That's why I don't wanna tell anything because I know you will try to solve things. I don't want you to feel frustrated around me and then leave me. I don't wanna lose you.

She wiped his tears.

I can never leave you like this Arnav.

she cut off the topic and said

"The coffee's getting cold."

She took him to the garden.

Let's have coffee here and trust me I will not force you if you're not comfortable with telling me anything, but I would really feel good if I could hear what you feel.

Your words never bother me, your silence does. In the past few days, what bothered me was why you're behaving strangely with me.

Aaisha, I don't know whom to thank, I never thought I could get someone like you in my life. Even, I'm filled with things now. I want relief but first let's finish the coffee. He smiled.

Uh yes! Let's go inside then. It's getting cold here, and you're already not well.

Um Aaisha, I know it might sound wrong to you but can you please stay in my room with me tonight? I just want to talk and be with you, nothing else.That too only if you are comfortable.

Umm, yeah sure! actually I am not feeling sleepy yet so, yes we can sit and talk.

Are you sure you're comfortable with me here?

Yes, no problem, I know I am safe around you.

I don't know when we both fell asleep but when I woke up in the morning the most beautiful thing was her, sleeping next to me. I couldn't take my eyes off her. She was looking so pretty. I was just staring, staring and staring.

She slightly moved and turned towards me. I was trying to put a blanket on properly but my movement woke her up.

"Good morning." She said softly.

Good morning! I can't believe it.

What?

You're next to me. I woke up next to you.

Haha ah well. She laughed.

By the way, how are you feeling now?

Absolutely amazing! I mean I am fine.

Hahaha yes, I can see that.

Ok Aaisha listen, get ready. I have so much to tell you today.

Sure, just give me half an hour and I will be ready.

She was getting ready and I went to prepare breakfast for us. I was nervous but I know what I have decided to do today is right.

Oh wow, someone's making breakfast. You know how to cook?

He laughed. Yeah a little.

I am impressed. Actually, I am very bad at cooking. You must have guessed last night when I made soup for you.

Hahaha. Oh no, that was delicious.

Come on. It wasn't but yeah at least, I can help you while cooking. Tell me what I should do.

Be with me.

He held my waist and pulled me closer. Moved my hair back from my neck then gently leaned and rested his head on my shoulder. Slightly kissed my neck.

Thank you so much for staying with me yesterday.

"Don't thank me Arnav, there's no need for this formality. You mean a lot to me." She said Softly. But then, immediately changed the topic as soon as she realised that her words are clearly indicating her feelings towards him. She looked away from him and said,

"I mean, I wanted to make sure you're fine. Now let's cook the food…. I am starving."

Alright! Can you pass me that ketchup?

Yup, here you go.

We laughed, talked, and looked at each other. We had the most amazing time even while preparing breakfast. Maybe, it's true that if you are with the right person you can be happy anywhere.

I should really appreciate your talent, this is delicious. So you can sing, write and cook too. How cool is that!

Aaisha, I thought about what you said to me last night and I think you really deserve to know everything about me now. Come let me show you something.

He took me to his room and showed me a diary.

What's this?

As I told you I write when I don't know how to express what I am feeling. It's a diary I wrote many things in. Songs, poetry or anything. These are all my music instruments. I feel better with all these around me. I try to express myself through singing too. Whenever I feel empty, I fill myself with all these things.

This is beautiful, I read a line or two, just wow. You love writing, don't you?

Actually, these are not just songs but I love to write anything that comes to mind. Sometimes it's a song, sometimes an article or poetry. In fact I love every form of art.. be it music, writing, dancing or paintings.. I believe a person who has hobbies is a person who has heart.

Arnav, what is this pain in your voice while talking about these? Your eyes are teary, you are looking disturbed.

Aaisha, the reason I am sad and the reason I was avoiding you after we stayed at that hotel is the same. I... I don't know how to say it. I..suffered severe depression, anxiety and much more. Actually I was too young when my parents got divorced, I grew up watching them fight. But when they decided to separate. My father said that he didn't want me so my mother got my custody. I lived with her. I saw how badly she had Been treated by her husband and I was too young to deal with that. I developed this habit of not trusting people. I used to be afraid of commitments. I always had this fear that something would happen and everyone would give up on me like my father did. If not, then I will have the same situation with my partner.

I don't know what I was feeling but there was something that wasn't right inside me. Even after being with people I felt like I don't connect properly with anyone I felt like no one understands me. No one will ever love me. So I started to write it or express it through things like music, writing, and all. I tried so much to be normal but these fears never really left me. I always feel like I am never good enough for anyone.. I try my best not to show it to the world but sometimes I feel hurt. I feel pain of what my mother had to go through. Clearly, she didn't have much but she gave me the best life.

I still feel the fear that people will leave me. I never shared anything with anyone ever, not even to my mom. But I always fought with these insecurities inside me.

I feel like I will never be good enough to love someone because... once I did. I loved someone, I tried to step into something I was most afraid of. But I still did it out of love for her.

There was someone I fell in love with. I tried my best to make her happy and give her a good life, I tried my best. There wasn't any moment where I would have disrespected her. Because I have seen my mother with that pain. But she broke with me which..which was hard to handle but what she said was worse, it scattered me. She said that I don't deserve love, nobody will ever love me. Aaisha, all these things broke me more and more. I started believing that no one will ever love me and I don't deserve any kind of love. I developed trust issues and I started feeling even worse. So there was a point where I thought I needed to fight with all these feelings, I tried it and undoubtedly it helped me a lot but even it couldn't get that fear out of me completely. So when I met you I can't tell you how I made myself believe that I have a person in my life who is so pure and loving. But suddenly all these things hit me and I thought I don't deserve you, you knew nothing about me and it felt wrong to give you any hopes without telling you the whole truth. I know people want a perfect partner, with zero flaws. While, I am the one who is filled with flaws, fears and doubts. I was even suicidal at a point in my life.

She wiped my tears with her soft and gentle hands and hugged me. I knew that she was in tears too. I hugged her back tightly..

Arnav, I am so sorry. I didn't know anything and I thought you don't want me anymore that's why you're being distant. Clearly, it's hard to tell what a person is going through by his or her face.

And how can you think that I will ever leave you because of your past or because of your insecurities. Do you really think I could ever use your past depression as an excuse to leave you? Arnav, relationship is about making it right together, growing together, evolving together and supporting each other together.

But Aaisha, I don't know if I am able to give you a life you deserve. I don't want to pull you to the dark side of my life.

We can find that bright side together. I know it's hard to tell someone about our insecurities or about our feelings. You shared it with me, thank you for at least considering telling me.

So you don't have any problems with the things I am still working on. Aaisha, I am still not over it properly and you know it might be a problem for you if we take anything forward. You have people around you who are normal and are ready to give you the world.

Yes, I am aware of everything you are indicating. First of all, what do you mean by normal? I don't see anything abnormal in you. I don't understand if suffering from fever or something once in a while is normal. Why is a person who is suffering from some insecurities or depression abnormal? Look, If I get a small wound then I will try to cure it. I will not call myself abnormal. And seriously, I don't look at it that way. If you look at it the way I see it, you will see a person who is perfect, who is loyal, honest, loving, caring and most importantly responsible. And as you said, you haven't overcame it completely yet, I don't have a problem with that either. My expectations from you are nothing but your presence and your honesty. Other than that I don't expect anything. You will always have me beside you holding your hand in any or every situation. And I get it, if You are not ready for a relationship yet. We can wait. I can wait as long as you feel something for me.

That's the issue Aaisha. I don't want you to suffer because of me but, I don't want to lose you either. I tried staying away from you but I couldn't.

Arnav, take your time. Think about it.

Really? You don't think something is wrong with me?

Hey no, I don't think that because there isn't anything wrong with you. It's normal.

Things you've experienced were bad, their impact was even worse and that's it. You will be fine, you will get through this and remember one thing, you do deserve love, you deserve everything.

I was already feeling better than ever, after knowing that she did not judge me. She did not leave me and she gave me time to recover. How can someone be such a beautiful person? But the only thing I was worried about was how I would recover and how much time it would take. I know she can wait for me but I don't want to keep her waiting for the love she deserves. She deserves the world and I wanna give it to her.

Aaisha! I know every girl has some expectations with the person she loves, don't you want anything in a relationship?

I don't have that many expectations in a relationship. But yes I do expect truth, respect and obviously love.

Uh.. do You mind if I take this call? It's a little urgent.

Oh take it no problem.

Someone called her and as soon as she read the name on the screen of her phone, she looked happy.

Oh my god what?

Really? Wow, I can't believe it.

She picked the call and I never heard her sound happier than this. I could see the joy in her smile like never before. She cut the call and looked at me, her beautiful eyes, my god! Her beauty mesmerises me every time I look at her.

You're looking happy, I would love to know the reason.

Oh yes I am very happy, you know my best friend is coming to live with me for a few days and I can't tell you how much I missed him. You know we have been friends since we were kids. I just love him. I want to introduce you to him.

Uh, nice! I would love to meet him too.

She was leaving the room. He slightly held her hand from the back to stop her. Pulled her closer, he slowly moved his hand to her waist, then hugged her from the back. She closed her eyes and was just feeling him, he hugged her even tightly, he kissed her cheek, then her neck, he gently kissed the back of her neck.

Uh Arnav, I think I should go now. You need to rest today.

She smiled and left the room pushing him back slightly.

How beautiful, how beautiful the stages of love are, how beautiful is it to find peace in someone's smile.

Hey! Hahaha don't avoid me like this.

"Don't tease me like this then." She said and laughed.

I went to her again and grabbed her not that gently this time. She was looking much more shy than before. I learned to kiss her, she put her hands around my neck then came a little closer, we were about to kiss.

Her phone rang!

Uh, I am sorry, I have to take it.

Yeah sure! It's fine.

She went to the other room to take that call and I sat on the couch waiting for her. I wasn't feverish but there was still some weakness.

Hey Arnav! You should sleep on the bed with a blanket on, it's cold here.

Oh I didn't know when I fell asleep. When did you come? Just now.

Oh! Is everything ok? It took you so long.

Yes everything is fine, that was just my friend I told you about.

Oh ok. Come let's sit together for a while.

We sat on the bed, she gave me the blanket. Then laid her head on my shoulder while talking to me.

We both fell asleep. When I got up she wasn't there.

Aaisha! Aaisha!

Yes, sorry I was on a call so I went out of the room because you were sleeping.

That's fine I was wondering where you are.

Arnav, actually I think I should leave now. I have already stayed here last night and it's evening now.

Uh, but you can stay here tonight too. I will drop you tomorrow morning if you want.

No actually, my friend will come tomorrow so I should reach home by today.

Ok if you want then I will drop you.

We sat in the car. I started driving but I didn't want to drop her. Even though we weren't talking, it was beautiful too. Even the silence feels like music when I am with her.

I don't know why I didn't want her to go. I wanted to stay with her longer. I don't know why everything feels right with her, I feel right with her.

Arnav, you can call me whenever you want. Don't stress much about anything ok? I'm here for you.

Means a lot, baby.

I got out to open the door. I wanted to hug her but I was worried about whether I was being too much to handle or should I just hug her without thinking about anything.

She held my hand.

Take care of yourself and just know that I will never leave you because of anything you told me.

She hugged me tightly.

Ah! I can't express how much it meant to me.

I hugged her back.

Hugging Arnav feels the best, I feel like I am at the safest place. His hands around my waist, what else do I need?

Thank you for everything Aaisha.

I was going Back to the car, I didn't want to go but...

Arnav! Uh actually I was thinking that my friend and I will go for a trip together once he's here so if you don't mind then you can join us, if you want we can call other friends too.

Uhh.. I would love to but are you sure?

Yes, in fact I was thinking if you are ok then you can stay here for a few days so that I can stay with my friend and take care of you at the same time. You had a fever just a day ago.

Uh ok if you're fine with.....

VI
Together

Oh my god! Oh what?? Yash!!!!

She ran to a guy and hugged him. She was looking happier than ever. The guy picked her up and was hugging her more and more.

Something in me was not comfortable with it, the way he was holding her. I felt like someone was touching something that belongs to me.

Yash, I can't believe it, you are here? You told me you will reach tomorrow.

Yes, because I wanted to surprise you. God! You don't know how much I missed this smile.

He hugged her again, wrapped his hands around her, she was holding him tight too, both were so happy. But I was just not feeling right. I was unable to understand why I felt strange.

Yash, I want you to meet someone.

Oh ok. Sure.

This is Arnav. My... uh my friend.

Hello Arnav.

Hello Yash!

Well what took you so long to call him a friend.?

Hey come on, don't trouble me.

Let's go inside guys, it's too cold here.

We went inside and she asked us to sit until she made coffee for us.

So Arnav, how do you know her?

Actually we met at a party which our mutual friend hosted.

Oh ok cool. So you are her friend now? Just friend right?

coffee is ready guys.... And tell me what you want to eat, I will order.

No, wait. Let me order something for us. Yash, I am thinking of ordering some white sauce pasta for myself. Are you ok with it or should I order something else for you?

Oh I love it so please order the same for me too.

Ok great then I am ordering it for all of us.

Hey, wait don't you know? Aaisha doesn't like it, she prefers red sauce pasta.

Uh I... I didn't know.

It's ok Arnav you will know about me with time.

She gave us the cups and sat beside me while talking to Yash. I was just looking at her and looking at Yash, noticing how different he is from me. He is indeed a wonderful guy, he is so lively and full of happiness, fun, excitement and above all, he knows Aaisha very well, better than me obviously.

Uh I am full now, thanks for the food Arnav.

It's ok Yash.

Aaisha, I am very tired and sleepy. I guess I am having jet lag. I am going to my room. Please wake me up tomorrow on time.

Alright. Goodnight.

Goodnight.

He went to one of the rooms as if he was fully familiar with the house. But I Didn't know which room I was supposed to stay in, so I asked her...

"Aaisha, where should I go? Can you please show me the room?"

Yes but there is only one room left so if you don't have any problem then we can share it.

Well I would love to.

I teased her a little as we didn't get a chance to talk that much about anything in front of Yash.

She smiled and my heart melted again. How beautiful is it when you have someone who is your strength and weakness at the same time.

Arnav I have placed a bottle of water beside your side of the bed and please let me know if you need anything.

She fell asleep as soon as she laid beside me, she was tired, as she was taking care of me last night and then took care of everything here too for Yash and I. I fell asleep too, holding her close to me. Her fragrance, her touch and her presence are the best things in the world.

My phone's alarm rang, for a second I almost forgot that I was not at my house.

I was so comfortable after a long time, I had someone who felt like home to me. I had someone who understands me.

When I woke up, she wasn't in the room.

I got up and went to the living room, she was there with Yash, they were laughing at something and I felt I had never seen Aaisha laughing her heart out like this before. I understand I am getting possessive about her and seeing him talking to her and laughing with her like that made me a little jealous. Seeing them like that together somewhere made me realise that what I feel for her is love and I would confess it directly before it's late.

Hey good morning guys.

Good morning Arnav!

So You slept comfortably last night?

Last night was Most comfortable of all.

Great! Arnav, actually, I am leaving for a meeting and I have already prepared breakfast for both of you.

Yash stood up and said, "Alright! Arnav and I will take care of your house, and after breakfast I too have some work lined up today so I guess I will be back tomorrow morning."

Oh? Tomorrow?

Yes, actually my meetings are in another city so it will take that much time but I will make sure from tomorrow all we will do is spend time together and have fun. By the way, all the best for your meeting today..

Thank you Yash, all the best to you too. bye Arnav.

I left for the meeting but my heart was not in my control. Arnav is all I think about these days.

How does a person who was a complete stranger just a couple months ago means so much to me now that I would do anything to see him happy

Love spreads like the sky

Float like clouds

Flows like the drops of water

Smells like the soil after rain

Feels like the cold wind

But,

Looks like only one person who stays in your heart...

Hello Aaisha where are you? I hope I didn't disturb you, I Wanted to talk about something important, that's why I called you.

Hello! That's totally fine. My meeting just got over, and now I'm heading back home but what happened?

Aaisha actually Arnav uh I don't know how to say.

What happened to Arnav? Say it. You are making me panic.

Aaisha, he went somewhere he was disturbed by something and we have been trying to contact him since morning but there is no clue. I thought he might have contacted you.

Chirag, what are you saying please tell me you all are just joking how can he suddenly go like this he was in a good mood when I left for work.

I know. He called me this morning and was very upset but he didn't tell the reason. Can you please try to call him and check if he picks up your call? You know he is still struggling with things. I hope he is not hurting himself in any way.

Ok I... will call him. I hope he is fine wherever he is.

Aaisha listen to me, do not panic, are you crying?

Chirag, I want to talk to him and make sure he is fine.

Ok try to call him and I will tell you if I get any clue.

Her heart was beating faster she was so worried that she couldn't stop her tears

She drove back home and called him hundreds of times but he didn't pick any, everyone started worrying even more as it was already midnight.

Aaisha was crying and crying messaging him calling him, asking people who he might have called but still got no clue of where he was

Then her phone rang and it was call from one of Arnav's friend

She grabbed the phone without a blink and picked the call

Hello? Have you talked you Arnav today? Do you know where is he?

Hello Aaisha.

Arnav?

Her heart skipped a beat, it was Arnav on the call.

Arnav, where are you? Why haven't you picked my calls and how could you just leave like this? Do you have any clue how much we all are worrying? You didn't even think about me before avoiding all of us like this?

Aaisha, listen, I am fine, don't worry I need some time.

Arnav, are you ok?

Arnav?

She started weeping. There was complete silence on the call. Both were silent.

Arnav please come back we will sort everything that's bothering you, just come back honey.

Aaisha, why do you want me to come back? Why are you worried about me like this?

First of all, stop crying and secondly, just come back right now if you consider me something to you, then come back.

Ok, but I don't want to meet anyone else.

Ok fine don't worry about that.

After talking to Arnav, it felt like I was finally breathing knowing that he was fine.

It's 3 AM But a question is still bothering her, what made him go like this.

Doorbell rang and without wasting a second, Aaisha ran carelessly to open the door. The moment she opened it, she bursted into tears and hugged him so tight that he could feel her heartbeat.

He controlled his tears and kissed her forehead.

She took him inside the house and there were millions of questions in her eyes but she wasn't able to ask any.

"I know....I... should not have left like this."

He said in a low and trembling voice controlling his emotions.

Yes, you should not have left like this, you should have talked to me before leaving and now you owe me at least an explanation of what this is all about.

I will but I have no courage to say it in words what I have been feeling all day so if you don't mind can we talk about it some other day please?

Fine! But we will definitely talk about it tomorrow.

She hugged him again.

Ah! I was so worried. And Arnav do you know.....

He kissed her, he wanted to pour all the love he was feeling for her. She kissed him back and he could feel her love, care and passion, his touch was making her feel the burn like never before and the heat of the moment was so strong that it was not in their control anymore to resist the physical love they both wanted to share. Her skin, his hands and their love.

And the night with Arnav was much more beautiful than she ever imagined. Her body was comfortable with him. He was in love with her heart and now her body too. It was beautiful, it was perfect. So perfect that his masculinity was wanting to bow down to her.

They both fell asleep after spending the most amazing night together.

The next morning she woke up with a noise in the kitchen.

Arnav? Are you in the kitchen?

She got up and went there, it was not Arnav but Yash.

Oh Yash? You?

Well yes it's me I told you yesterday, I will be back by tomorrow. Wait, were you expecting someone else?

Actually, I thought it's Arnav.

Oh I see. You are looking... happy what happened?

"Nothing," she said. but her face was explaining it all.

You are blushing.. ok I got it.

He laughed.

Uh Yash, have you seen Arnav?

Yes he went somewhere as soon as I got here.

Oh ok.

She did not expect him to leave like this, she wanted him to stay with her a longer.

Oh! see Arnav is calling me.

A big smile came on her face after seeing his name on the screen of her phone.

Hello Arnav!

Hi Aaisha, I am really sorry I had to leave before you woke. Actually it was something important and I hope you don't mind.

No, after this call I will not mind it, that's fine, take care.

Sure! Love you.

Love you more.

That call changed her mood instantly and it was really hard for her to be upset with him.

His voice can light my mood up within seconds.

Yash, I am super hungry. Let's have breakfast. Did you make something?

Yes I did. Everything that you love is on the dining table, come let's have it.

She was looking so beautiful, her messy bun and a loose shirt, shorts, and the most beautiful thing about her, her smile.

Yash was sitting in front of her and for a moment he was so lost he did not realise he was staring at her.

Hey, the food is amazing man. You are an awesome cook.

Hey thanks. So how was your day without me yesterday?

To be honest, it was really very bad, but ended up beautifully so, it was quite like a roller coaster.

Okay.... I guess I know how it must have ended but don't you think Aaisha you are trusting this guy a little early?

Um, but I thought you liked him too. As far as I know, he is a nice guy and I guess I am falling for him.

I am just saying you should not trust him this soon but anyway, it's your call and all I want is to see you happy so don't mind what I said.

Oh not at all, you are my best friend, you have all the right to give your opinion.

Her day passed while thinking about him, about the love she has already developed for Arnav, the love she still has to give to him, his name, his eyes, his voice and above all, his heart. Everything about him is just perfect and beautiful.

She was missing him more and more.

While Arnav was drowning in his own thoughts, his heart was heavy and eyes were filled with words that he didn't share with anyone.

Should I tell Aaisha the truth or not? Will that hurt her? She will surely think that I am making excuses and I am betraying her. But if I run from her like this, this might hurt her even more after whatever happened.

Arnav was in the midst of different thoughts.

Thoughts....it's weird how lost sometimes we can feel in our own mind, How much pain can we feel because of our own thoughts, mind and heart

She was feeling on the top of the world with the most beautiful feeling in the word that is love. She was in love with everything about him, His eyes, his smile, His touch, the excitement with which he talks about things he likes. She was in love with the way his eyes express everything before he actually says anything.

"Arnav, I can't wait to tell you how much I love you."

She said to herself.

It was already midnight while waiting, Aaisha was now worried whether Arnav is okay or not.

I am pretty sure Arnav is not fine, there is something he is hiding inside him from me while pretending to be happy. He went somewhere without telling anyone a day before too and now again.

I can't sit and wait for him to come back to me like nothing happened.

VII
Tussle

Yash! Yash?

Yes Aaisha, sorry I was on a call, I didn't hear when you called me.

It's ok, actually I am going to Arnav's house don't worry if I will be late.

But Aaisha, why do you want to go there? That guy doesn't care about you at all, don't waste your time on that person.

"Yash! I love him and I can't leave him like this. I know he does care, he has infinite love in his heart for everyone. The only thing is that he doesn't show it that much. I know him. He is one of the most real people I have ever seen and I don't understand why you don't wanna see the good in him?"

Aaisha asked him furiously.

"Because there is no good in him. Do you get it?"

Yash shouted and went out of the room slamming the door.

Her eyes were filled with tears and heart was filled with the love she had for Arnav. The brain wanted to trust everything that Yash said.

She went to Yash again.

Yash, I know you care about me and that's why you don't want to see me with him because since the day you have came, all you saw is him acting like he doesn't care about me but there is a side of him that I have seen and I want to hold on to that side of him.

Aaisha, you know I care about you and I can't see you hurting yourself for someone, ok I get it that you saw something in him which might be worth holding on to. But, have you ever asked yourself the reason why I care so much about you and why can't I see you sad even for a minute? Have you ever asked yourself why I want to see you happy? Why is it only you I share everything to? Why is it only you I wanna be around all the time? Do you have any idea how much it hurts to love someone who doesn't love you back? You don't have any idea of it and that's the only reason I don't want you to feel the pain that I feel every time when I see you loving him not me. When I see you loving the person who is not here and you are not noticing the love of this guy who is standing right here with you.

She was shocked for a moment, she couldn't say anything on this for a few seconds, it felt as if her heart got injured badly. Yash's intense stare was plucking her heart out.

Yash you.... you never told me this. Her voice was trembling.

You never noticed Aaisha.

Uh...... Yash I respect you and your feelings so much but, I don't feel the same way for you.

You are my family but I don't see a life partner in you. I see that in him Yash.

He made me feel the way I never felt, I wasn't ready to feel like this ever and he showed me that choosing me is not hard.

You will always be my family but....

It's ok Aaisha, I don't want to be selfish with you, if you want him, if you really want to put efforts to make it work, I will support you and just know that I will not let you hurt yourself in this process ok?

She smiled and hugged him.

He hugged him back tightly, she could feel friendship winning.

The friend in him defeated the person who was crushing over her.

Ok now, get off. Do not make me feel emotional ok?

She looked at him with a warm smile and said, "I should go to see him. Thank you for making me feel heard, Yash."

She went to her car and something was telling her that her trust on Arnav is not a waste, he is the best person for her.

How unexpected life can get sometimes,

We can do things for someone we love that we would never do for anyone. No matter what the situation might be, no matter how dark it gets, we try to look for that one ray of hope to hold on, just because of one single reason. LOVE.

Aaisha reached his house and saw the door open, it was windy, cold, silent but her heart was filled with chaos.

She got into the house and her heart skipped a beat again, seeing him singing his heart out, just like before.

His deep voice, the visible veins on his neck while singing, his perfection in playing guitar, the lyrics and the purity in his eyes. How can someone not love him?

How can someone know him and not feel passionate and lost in love for him?

His presence, his aura, his honesty, his innocence.

She was just looking at him, stunned by his aura and lost in his love.

He was lost in the world of music, love and passion or maybe it was all her in his mind

Aaisha? When did you get here?

He put his guitar aside and grabbed her in his arms the moment he saw her there.

Her warmth, his scent, her care, his passion and their love.

Arnav! I want to…

I know Aaisha. I let you down every time you trust me, and I did that again.

You never let me down Arnav. I know your intentions are nothing but pure. I just wanna know everything this time, don't hide, don't lie, I want the complete truth. Can I at least expect this?

You have every right to ask this and I promise I will not lie this time, I will not hide anything. You can ask me anything you want.

Why did you leave like this Yesterday? Then today you came here before I woke up, why? Is there anything that you are not telling me?

before he could say anything His eyes filled with tears.

She held his hand and said. "I am here and will always be here by your side. Trust me, nothing can change what I feel for you. No matter how big the issue is."

That's the reason Aaisha, I don't want you to be with me.

What? Why are you saying this? Did I do something wrong?

Hey no no, that's not what I mean. Actually my ex girlfriend called me yesterday, I didn't have her number saved so I picked up that call. She was drunk and she asked me to get back with her. I told her that I don't love her anymore. I have someone else in my life then she said that.....

That? Say it Arnav.

She said that I am a terrible person to be with my childhood traumas and my insecurities makes it worse for people to be with me, I ruin things wherever I go, she said that I should not be with anyone because I don't deserve someone's love, my insecurities are nothing but the biggest turn off.

So, I don't know why it disturbed me so much. I didn't want to talk to anyone and I went to spend time alone, I ran from the situation like I always do but then something pulled me back again. I couldn't leave you, I feel that peace around you which I never felt before I don't feel judged when you are around so, I came back to you last night and trust me it is the most precious moment for me I didn't want to make you feel that I left you and trust me I didn't leave today, I wanted to gift you something as a thank you for giving me the best moments so I was leaving to buy something for you but then I met Yash and he said it too, that I should not ruin your life by being in it, He said that you deserve someone like him not like me. He even said that I'm using you. Aaisha I swear, I never thought of it this way. I....

Arnav, look at me, I came here, why? Because I feel something for you, because I know that you are worth it. Do you really think you are ruining my life by being in it? Do you know what I feel? I feel blessed to have you in my life and I don't have any words to describe this feeling. Why do you run from people who love you? Just because someone said something stupid to you, you believed it?

Aaisha... I don't know what it is that I feel whenever someone says things that I am afraid of. My whole life I have been feeling abandoned by people I love, it broke me so much that I started believing there's something wrong with me. I was trying so hard to get through this and overcome these feelings for a long time and it was working. I overcame a lot but when someone says this directly to me all my wounds start bleeding again. I realised that I am not over it fully and I don't deserve to be in your life. I don't know why I feel like this again and again, all I know is I have never received the love you give me. So, I feel like I don't deserve to be loved like this.

Tears were dripping from his eyes while saying all this to her.

She wiped his tears with her soft hands and said,

"Arnav! You are wrong here, totally wrong. Just because you never received the love doesn't mean you don't deserve it, in fact you deserve much more than this. I totally understand that you are still fighting with your own thoughts somewhere but that can not stop me from loving you, we all deserve love and care, it's just your life was a little more cruel with you till now and I am completely aware with your insecurities, your feelings and your heart which carries nothing but love and I promise you we will get through it together, people neglect problems like this, I know many people think that being insecure about something isn't something worth dealing but I know how hard it is to deal with your own mind and thoughts, we all have insecurities about things and it's totally normal. You don't have to run from any situation anymore, we can deal with everything together Arnav. You deserve it all. Don't let yourself get affected by something people say out of jealousy or hate."

Whenever I talk to you Aaisha, I feel like you are the best decision I have ever made in my life. How can you be so supporting and understanding even though I haven't done anything for you?

Who said you haven't? Don't you think being loyal to someone no matter what the circumstances are, is more than enough for a person like me.

So are you ok now? Or do you want me to say a few more good things about you because I can but I am super tired now, I am speaking from the past ten minutes continuously Arnav. Then she laughed.

Seeing her happy is an out of the world feeling for me, her purity, her simplicity, her support, her love and even her Anger. Everything about her is just beautiful and soothing. How beautifully she makes me forget every bad memory that I have been fighting with for years, without making me feel worthless.

Thank you so much for everything Aaisha.

You know what I don't like? Thank you and sorry. If you really want to make it then let's go and eat something because I am super hungry.

Ok sure, let's go.

He leaned and kissed her, she held him softly by placing her hands on his jaw.

None of them wanted to stop kissing each other but then Aaisha stepped back and blushed.

Hey are you still blushing? Even after....

(he teased her)

Ok stop it Arnav, let's go.

Yup ok I get it, don't be shy let's go to that restaurant where we first went.

He took her to that restaurant and couldn't stop looking at her the whole time. Her beauty is indeed irresistible.

They were having dinner together again at the same place from where it all started.

Hey Aaisha, it's your birthday this weekend, is there anything specific that I can give you which you might like? Because I am very bad at these things.

Well I don't need anything other than you sitting with me, but if you are insisting that much, you can cook something for me because I love your cooking.

Haha! Alright. I will surely cook something good for you. Well there is something else that I want to give to you.

What's that?

I am not gonna tell you before your birthday.

Hey that's wrong, please tell me.

Nope. He laughed.

Fine! But this is wrong. It's so hard to be patient.

I will try my best to make sure it's worth the wait.

Thank you Arnav.

For? I haven't given you anything yet.

No. Actually, this thanks is for telling me everything and now for this wonderful dinner. You trusted me with your life story, which means a lot to me.

He gave her a smile and said, "you mean the world to me so you deserve to know everything about me."

Ok don't make blush now,

I think we should go back home because it's getting late.

They drove back home.

Aaisha, you go to sleep. I have some work to finish so I will be in the living room. By the way, where is your friend?

He went for some office work again.

Um ok good night.

Yup! Sleep well.

VIII
Written

Three days went by in a blink of an eye and I am trying my best to take care of Aaisha. With her I am feeling better everyday. It's her birthday within a few minutes and I want her to be the happiest today.

Aaisha! Come closer.

He was lying beside her and pulled her close.

He slightly went close to her ear and whispered.

Happy Birthday Sweetheart. I hope I can wish you like this every year.

He kissed her softly.

Thank you so much Arnav. I wish that too.

So Aaisha, you should attend the calls and messages. I should sleep now. I have to wake up early tomorrow.

Sure, sleep well.

I woke up and saw my room decorated beautifully. Before I could get off the bed Arnav came into the room with a beautiful bouquet in his hand.

Happy birthday to the most amazing person I know!

And this is for you.

He handed over the red roses bouquet to me.

I hugged him and like always, his scent makes me forget about every other thing.

Aaisha, here's your dress, get ready fast I wanna take you somewhere.

Oh my god! this dress, it's pretty.

Glad you liked it. Come on, get ready.

I went out of the room, I don't know why I am getting nervous. I just hope she likes it.

She came out of the room wearing that dress, my heart skipped a beat for a while. Her eyes, deeper than the ocean, I wanted to hide her in my eyes, I wanted to feel her, look at her, touch her. I lost my heart and found her at that place.

How to tell her that my life is all about her now, I want to be with her for the rest of my life, I wanted to tell her that I know I am not the best person but I am yours now. I never believed in god but when I look at her I feel like god gave me the most precious person to me.

Absolutely gorgeous! My god! It's hard to take my eyes off you Aaisha.

Thank you Arnav. The dress is really very beautiful.

You are welcome,

I Can't wait to start the celebration Aaisha let's go.

I took her to the party that I hosted for her, though I was worried about whether she would like it or not.

And the Birthday girl is here guys!!!!!

Arnav announced the party he hosted for me, all of my friends, my family were there, my favourite songs were playing in the background and the party hall was decorated so beautifully, just the way I like it. I never imagined that this is going to be so perfect.

Did you like it Aaisha?

Arnav, it all feels like a dream. This is just wow. I am speechless. Thank you so much. Your surprise made my day.

Well that's not all, the main surprise is still waiting for you.

What? There is something else?

Yes, there is.

He held my hand and took me to that beautifully decorated stage, I was getting nervous, it was all dreamy. The stage, the people, the songs.

He took the mic and said.

"Aaisha, first of all a very happy birthday to you. You are looking gorgeous.

Seriously you are the best person I know, you made me realise that I can be loved and respected. Your presence in my life worked as a lucky charm for me. And this is the best day to officially admit that

I LOVE YOU and I want to spend every day of my life with you. I want to call you mine in front of the world. So, here before asking you about your feelings for me, I want to give you a little gift which is very close to my heart, to admire you for being with me in my highs and lows."

Arnav's words were so pure and deep it was hard to believe it's happening for real. He was saying the words I was dying to hear from him. And before I could say anything he brought a book to me.

Aaisha, I want to give you this book.

Oh god! Arnav this book has your name written on it as a writer. Wow! You wrote a book?

Yes, it's my first book. It's very close to my heart, it's about how a person who came into my life like an angel, who healed me, who loved me without any condition, whose presence felt like a blessing in my life, who made me understand that it's possible to overcome traumas, insecurities and sadness, who never insulted me or made me feel bad for feeling the way I feel, who loved me for who I am.

It's about a person who cured me. So I wanted to give the first copy of this book to that person herself. You literally are the cure of sadness in my life. You read my eyes, you read the things I was hiding inside me and when I look into your eyes all I see is love, passion and kindness. How strange is it? You read the truth of my feelings even while I was showing lies in my eyes, you are so pure that everything you feel lies in your eyes.

That's what you named it Arnav, lies in the eyes. Beautiful!

They both were trying hard not to cry....

Then Arnav looked into her eyes, held her hands and asked,

Aaisha, Do you feel the same love that I feel for you? Will you be mine forever?

With tears of joy in her eyes and with a beautiful smile, she said YES!